OLIVIA™
Takes a Trip

adapted by Ellie O'Ryan
based on the screenplay "OLIVIA Takes a Road Trip"
written by Eric Shaw
illustrated by Jared Osterhold

Ready-to-Read

Simon Spotlight
New York   London   Toronto   Sydney

Based on the TV series *OLIVIA*™ as seen on Nickelodeon™

SIMON SPOTLIGHT
An imprint of Simon & Schuster Children's Publishing Division
1230 Avenue of the Americas, New York, New York 10020
Copyright © 2010 Silver Lining Productions Limited (a Chorion company). All rights reserved.
OLIVIA™ and © 2010 Ian Falconer. All rights reserved.
All rights reserved, including the right of reproduction in whole or in part in any form.
SIMON SPOTLIGHT, READY-TO-READ,and colophon are registered trademarks of Simon & Schuster, Inc.
For information about special discounts for bulk purchases, please contact Simon & Schuster
Special Sales at 1-866-506-1949 or business@simonandschuster.com.
Manufactured in the United States of America 0916 LAK
12 13 14 15 16 17 18 19 20
Library of Congress Cataloging-in-Publication Data
Bryant, Megan E.
Olivia takes a trip / adapted by Megan E. Bryant ; illustrated by Jared Osterhold. — 1st ed.
p. cm. — (Ready-to-read)
"Based on the screenplay 'Olivia Takes a Road Trip' written by Eric Shaw."
"Based on the TV series 'Olivia' as seen on Nickelodeon"—T.p. verso.
I. Osterhold, Jared, ill. II. Olivia (Television program) III. Title.
PZ7.B83980l 2010
[E]—dc22
2009029213
ISBN 978-1-4424-1381-8 (hc)
ISBN 978-1-4169-9933-1 (pbk)

Olivia and her family
are taking a trip.
Olivia is excited to fly
on a plane!

Olivia packs her trunk.
She packs clothes and
her favorite toy.

Ian packs a small
lunch box.
"This is my suitcase!"
Ian says.

Dad has some bad news.

A big storm is coming.

The plane cannot fly

in the storm.

They will drive the car
to Grandma's house
instead.

Olivia is sad.

She wanted to fly
on a plane!

Julian comes over
to say good-bye.

He has a present for Olivia.

It is a walkie-talkie!

Olivia and her family
get in the car.

"Are we there yet?" Ian asks.

The walkie-talkie is lou

It wakes up William!

William starts to cry.

Olivia wishes she were
on a plane.

The car ride is boring.

At the gas station Olivia helps Dad wash the windshield.

Dad's brush has soap on it.

Olivia's brush is muddy.

Dad has to wash the

windshield again!

Mom buys an ice pop for
Olivia and Ian to share.
Olivia wants the red part.
Ian wants the red part too!

The ice pop lands on the car.
Dad has to wash the
windshield again.
"We will never get
to Grandma's house!"
Olivia says.

Olivia has an idea.

She will imagine that

she is on a plane!

"Welcome to Air Olivia!"
Captain Olivia says.

Olivia's plane has a movie
for Dad to watch.
And popcorn for Dad to eat.
There is a yummy dinner
for Mom.

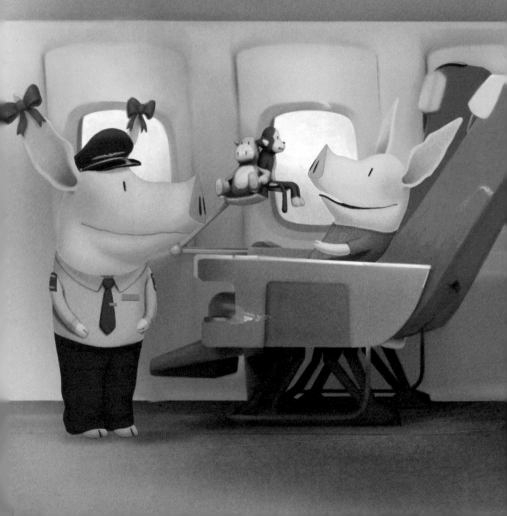

And a red rose for Mom, too.

"This is the best plane ever!"

Mom says.

Captain Olivia tells her family to put on their seat belts.

Captain Olivia sees dark clouds out the window.

"Uh-oh!" says Olivia.
"Dark clouds mean
a storm is coming."

"We will fly around the storm," Captain Olivia says. The plane loops around a rainbow.

It flies past the storm!

"We are at Grandma's
house!" Olivia shouts.
She gives Grandma
a big hug.